# THIS BOOK IS HAUNTED

*In loving memory of my mother,*
*Adele Rocklin*
*—J.R.*

*To my Mom and Dad*
*—J.A.*

An I Can Read Book™

# THIS BOOK IS

# HAUNTED

by
## Joanne Rocklin

pictures by
## JoAnn Adinolfi

HarperCollins*Publishers*

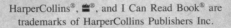
This Book Is Haunted
Text copyright © 2002 by Joanne Rocklin
Illustrations copyright © 2002 by JoAnn Adinolfi
Printed in the U.S.A. All rights reserved.
www.harperchildrens.com

Library of Congress Cataloging-in-Publication Data
Rocklin, Joanne.
   This book is haunted / by Joanne Rocklin ; pictures by JoAnn Adinolfi.
      p.       cm. — (An I can read book)
   Summary: This book's "not too scary" ghost host tells six spooky stories.
   ISBN 0-06-028456-0 — ISBN 0-06-028457-9 (lib. bdg.)
   [1. Ghosts—Fiction.   2. Halloween—Fiction.   3. Haunted houses—Fiction.]
I. Adinolfi, JoAnn, ill.   II. Title.   III. Series.
PZ7.R59 Tf   2001                                          00-047956
[E]—dc21

1  2  3  4  5  6  7  8  9  10
❖
First Edition

# Contents

This book is haunted!

By me.

Wait!

Do not close this book.

I will not scare you.

Much.

I know you like stories.

I will tell you some scary ones.

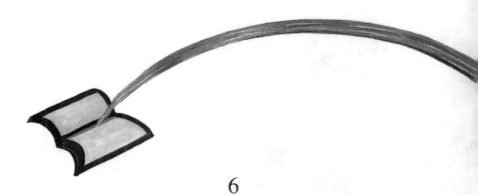

# 105 Windy Street

On Halloween Eve

Pam and Flo put on their costumes.

"We need bigger bags

for our candy," said Pam.

"Much bigger," said Flo.

Pam and Flo found two great big bags.

"Be home by seven o'clock!"

said their mother.

"Candy sweet!

Candy chewy!

Candy sweet!

Candy gooey!"

sang Pam and Flo.

The girls knocked on door after door.

"Trick or treat!" they said.

People put candy

into their great big bags.

After a while

Flo looked at her watch.

"It is seven o'clock.

We should go home now," Flo said.

"But our bags are not full!

I want more candy!" said Pam.

"Okay," said Flo.

"Let's try one more house."

Pam and Flo knocked

at 105 Windy Street.

A witch and a ghost opened the door.

"Neat costumes!" said Pam.

"I'm glad you think so,"

said the ghost.

"Trick or treat?" asked Flo.

"We have no treats,"

said the witch.

"But we know some tricks!"

said the ghost.

"Watch this."

"EEK!" shouted Pam and Flo.

They dropped

their great big bags of candy

and ran all the way home.

"Candy sweet!
Candy chewy!
Candy sweet!
Candy gooey!"
sang the witch and the ghost.

# Baby Bibble

Sally Bibble loved to draw
every single thing she saw.

Baby Bibble

loved to scribble.

Halloween sky,

Halloween moon,

skeletons, goblins,

witch on a broom,

vampires, ghosts,

big, black cat—

Sally Bibble

drew all that.

17

Next she took a special pen,

and she counted one to ten.

Then Sally drew a little scribble

that looked a lot like Baby Bibble.

They never found her baby sister.

Sally Bibble hardly missed her.

# Tap, Tap, Tap

"Do you hear that?"

asked one brother to another.

"Hear what?"

"Hear *that*!"

TAPPITY TAPPITY TAPPITY
TAP!

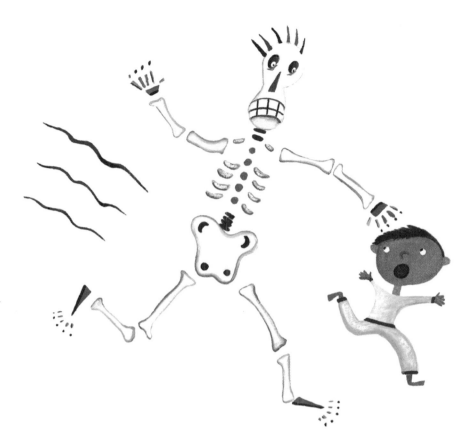

"What could it be?"

asked the smaller of the two.

"Well," said the bigger brother,

"it could be a skeleton

coming after you!

21

"Or it could be a mummy
waking up from a nap
looking for a snack."
TAP!
TAP!
TAP!

"What could *that* be?"

asked the smaller of the two.

"Well," said the bigger brother,

"it could be a monster

tapping with its claw,

the scariest monster

you ever saw!"

TAPPITY TAP!

The big brother said,
"It doesn't scare *me*!
It's just a little branch
from the apple tree!"
"Just a little branch
from the apple tree?"
asked the smaller brother.

# SNAP!

"See?" said the big brother.

"Just a little branch

from the apple tree."

The smaller brother said,

"Good night."

The bigger brother said,

"Sleep tight."

**TAP! TAP! TAP!**

# House for Rent

"What a nice house!" said Mrs. Green.

"Let's rent it," said Mr. Green.

"That house is haunted," said a man.

"Silly!" said Mrs. Green.

"There is no such thing

as a haunted house."

"Oh, no? Listen to this," said the man.

"HELLO!" shouted the man.

"*HELLO!*" something shouted back.

"That is just an echo,"

said Mrs. Green.

"All empty houses have echoes."

The next day the movers came.

"The sofa and the chair

go here," said Mr. Green.

*"GO HERE!"* said the echo.

"The table and the stove

go there," said Mrs. Green.

*"GO THERE!"* said the echo.

"The bed and the lamp
go here," said Mr. Green.
"*GO HERE!*" said the echo.
"And all of the books
go here and there," said Mrs. Green.

"*GO HERE AND THERE!*"
said the echo.

"Now our house is not empty,"

said Mrs. Green.

"No more echoes,"

said Mr. Green.

"What a nice house!"

said Mrs. Green.

*"I THINK SO, TOO!"*

said the echo.

33

# Witch's Stew

Dead black bugs

Pickles and glue

Skeleton bones

A pumpkin head, too

Monsters' teeth

A smelly old shoe

All in a pot

For our witch's stew.

SLURP!

Delicious!

Now all we need

Is someone like you—

To help us eat our witch's stew!

# The Story of Bill

Once there was

a boy named Bill.

Bill was mean.

37

He stole desserts.

He hogged the TV.

He never shared the sofa

with his sister.

(She had to sit on the floor.)

Bill's sister was reading

a library book.

It was due back on October 31.

"This book is scary!"

said Bill's sister.

Bill stole the book.

He read it that night.

"This book is not so scary!"

he said.

Bill hid the book under his bed.

On October 31 Bill's sister asked,

"Where is my book?"

"Who knows?" said Bill.

"My book is due!" said his sister.

"Who cares?" said Bill.

Bill dressed like a pirate

for Halloween.

He came home with lots of candy.

He ate all of it that night.

He ate most of his sister's, too.

Then he went to bed.

Suddenly

Bill heard something.

"My book is due!"

whispered a voice in the dark room.

"Who cares?" said Bill.

"My book is due!"

said the voice again.

Bill shivered.

He quivered.

"Who is under my bed?" Bill asked.

"MY BOOK IS DUE!"

shouted the voice.

It was a creepy, weepy voice.

Bill put his pillow over his head.

"Who are you?" Bill cried.

**H**ere I am again,

in *your* book.

Wait!

Do not close it!

Why don't you read it again?

Or maybe you could

share it with a friend.

Maybe you could

tell *me* a story or two.

Ghosts get lonely, you know.

So I hope this is not

**THE END!**